characters created by

lauren child

Say Cheese!

dial books for young readers

Charlie and Lola™

Text based on the script
written by Samantha Hill

Illustrations from the TV animation

produced by Tiger Aspect

First published in the United States by
DIAL BOOKS FOR YOUNG READERS
A division of Penguin Young Readers Group
Published by The Penguin Group
Penguin Group (USA) Inc., 375 Hudson Street, New York, NY 10014, U.S.A.
Penguin Group (Canada), 90 Eglinton Avenue East, Suite 700, Toronto, Ontario, Canada M4P 2Y3 (a division of Pearson Penguin Canada Inc.)
Penguin Books Ltd, 80 Strand, London WC2R 0RL, England
Penguin Ireland, 25 St. Stephen's Green, Dublin 2, Ireland (a division of Penguin Books Ltd)
Penguin Group (Australia), 250 Camberwell Road, Camberwell, Victoria 3124, Australia (a division of Pearson Australia Group Pty Ltd)
Penguin Books India Pvt Ltd, 11 Community Centre, Panchsheel Park, New Delhi - 110 017, India
Penguin Group (NZ), Cnr Airborne and Rosedale Roads, Albany, Auckland 1310, New Zealand (a division of Pearson New Zealand Ltd)
Penguin Books (South Africa) (Pty) Ltd, 24 Sturdee Avenue, Rosebank, Johannesburg 2196, South Africa
Penguin Books Ltd, Registered Offices: 80 Strand, London WC2R 0RL, England
Published in Great Britain by Puffin Books

Manufactured in China on acid-free paper
1 3 5 7 9 10 8 6 4 2
Library of Congress Cataloging-in-Publication Data
Child, Lauren.
Say cheese! / characters created by Lauren Child ; [text based on the script written by Samantha Hill ; illustrations from the TV animation produced by Tiger Aspect].
p. cm.
ISBN-13: 978-0-8037-3095-3
I. Charlie and Lola (Television program) II. Title.
PZ7.C4383Say 2007
[E]—dc22
2006102579

I have this little sister Lola.
She is small and very funny.
Today the school photographer is coming
and it is Lola's first ever school photo.

Lola says,
   "Mum said it is going to be
an EXTREMELY special photograph.
      Especially if I stay all tidy and clean."

                     I say,
               "And how easy do you
                  think THAT will be, Lola?"

                  "It'll be easy peasy,
            lemon squeezy," says Lola.

"I can be really **tidy** and **clean**
for my school **photograph**. I can, Charlie.
Look at all these **photographs** on holiday
at Granny and Grandpa's."

"I didn't get
chocolate on my dress!"
says Lola.

I say,
"No, not on your
dress, Lola..."

"What about this one
in the park?"

Lola says,
"But I didn't get
my shoes dirty!"

"No, that's because you
took them off, Lola!"

"And look at your hair in this one."

Lola says,
"My face is all clean ...
and look at my big
smile. Mum always says
I'm a good smiler!"

I say,
"Yep, you're a great
smiler ... and what do you say
for a big smile?"

Lola says,

"Say Cheese! Cheese!
Cheese!"

When it's time to go to school,
Lola says,
"Mum and me found my nicest skirt
and these are my best shoes
and my favorite hairclips.

So you see, Charlie,
it will be a lovely
school photograph."

On the playground, Lola sees Lotta.
Lola says,
"On the way to school I didn't even splash
in one single puddle."

"Neither did I!" says Lotta.

"I think I will look like the most tidiest person
in the school photograph,"
says Lola.

"Yes, you will,"
says Lotta,
"maybe..."

"Come on, Lotta," says Lola.
"Let's just play one
game of puddles."
Lotta says,
"I told my mum I would not
jump in any puddles."

"OK then," says Lola. "Let's play run around the puddles."

"See, when you run around you can stay all nice and clean!"

Then the bell goes for the start of school.

In the classroom, Lola says,
"I like my book. Do you like your book, Lotta?"
"Yes, but I do like the water tray too."

Lola says, "But reading is more tidy."
Lotta says, "Maybe we could play with something else?"

Then Lola says,
"What about the water tray?"

"Yes, yes, yes!"

Lotta says,
"Water doesn't make you
messy, does it?"

Lola says,
"No, water makes
you **clean**."

At lunchtime, Lola says,
"Now I'm going
        to drink my pink milk,

very,
    very
        carefully."

"Oh no!"

Back in the classroom, Lola says,
"I love painting."

"Me too," says Lotta. "It is my best thing.
I'm sure we can stay all clean
with our aprons on."

"I'm sure too," says Lola.
    "Just one finger each."

    "Careful, Lola..."

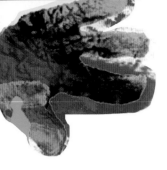
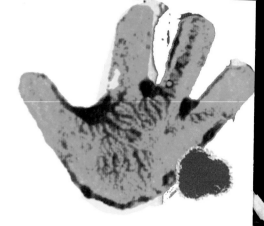

Then Lola says,
"Urgh...Lotta, my hands
are all blue."

And Lotta says,
    "My hands are a bit
green and a bit red."

"But paint washes off,
    doesn't it?" says Lola.

    "Oh yes!" says Lotta.
        "Paint washes off!"

When Lotta goes to
    wash her hands,
Lola says,
    "I just want to
have one look
    at my lovely
painting!"

Then it's time
for the school photo.

"Wait, Lotta!
I MUST have clean hands!"
says Lola.

"Wait for me!"

When we're waiting for our turn
to have our **photo** taken,

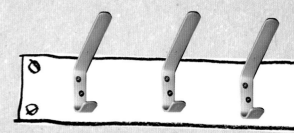

Lola says,
"Look how **clean** my hands
are, Charlie."

I say, "Just remember to **smile**."

"Oh yes," says Lola,
"I nearly forgot...I'm a good **smiler!**"

Then it's our turn.

I say, "Stay still, Lola.
Stop wriggling. Ready?"

"Whoops!" says Lola.

Then I say,
"And again. Ready,

1...
   2...
      3...!"

"Oh!" says Lola.

"Cheeese!"

Later, we look at
our school photographs.
I say, "Well, at least you're smiling, Lola!"

"But I'm NOT clean and I'm NOT tidy,
and I did try."

Lola says, "I just wanted one photograph so Mum would be pleased."

"But Mum will be pleased," I say.

Lola says, "But I wanted Mum to be pleased because I was all tidy and clean."

And then I have an idea...

Dad says we can use
some of the old photos...

After lots of

cutting

and snipping

and sticking,

Lola and I say...

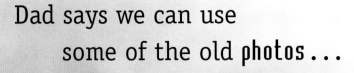

"There!"

At bedtime, Lola comes into our room
with the special photo.

I say, "What did Mum say?"

"Mum says I REALLY am
a VERY good smiler,"
says Lola.

"Cheese!"